Speedway Rider

Contents

1

'Come On You Reds!'

It was the two-minute warning.
'All riders to the start … all riders to the start.'

Out of the pits zoomed the motorbikes.
The crowd gave a cheer.
Under the big floodlights
the home team's red colours shone brightly.
Far back in the crowd
Wesley leaned forward to get a better view.

'Come on you Reds,' he shouted.
'Red for victory,' shouted his mate Rob
standing next to him.
The starting marshall waved his arms.
The bikes came to the starting tape.
Any second now the race would begin.
The bike engines roared.
All the riders were very still.

Wesley loved this moment best.
There was everything to play for.
Nothing was settled.
In a split second the bikes would zoom away.
The riders were desperate to be first away.
They would go flat out into the first bend.

The green light flashed on.
The engines roared even louder.
Up went the tape. Off went the bikes.
Up flew the dirt behind them in great showers.
The bikes were neck and neck.
Nobody was clearly in front.

Now the first bend was in sight.
A blue bike was just going in front.
Its rider leaned into the bend.
The bike was at an angle to the track.
Its back tyre gripped the dirt.
An even bigger shower of dirt shot in the air.
The rider held the bike low to the track.
His leg touched the track as the bike slithered
and skidded round the bend.
The bike was round the bend now.

The rider pulled the bike upright.
His hand turned the throttle.
The long straight part of the track
was ahead. The bike went faster.
Much much faster.
It went up to 70 mph in three seconds.
The bike had no brakes.
Its rider showed no fear.
Then it was into the second bend.
The blue bike was well in front now.
The back wheel bit into the dirt
clear of the rest.

'Another Blue victory,' said Rob.
'The race isn't finished yet,' said Wesley.
But he knew the blue bike should win.
Only an accident or a huge effort
from the bike in second place
could stop its victory.

'Another bad night for the Reds,'
said Rob ripping up his race card.
'Another wasted night.'
'Give them a chance,' said Wesley.
'I have given them a chance,' said Rob.
'We come down here week after week
and they always lose.'

'It's still a great night out,' said Wesley.
'The best night of the week.'
'Not any more,' said Rob.
'I'm done with speedway.'

2

The Chicken Chaser

Wesley had a part time job.

He delivered pizzas on a motorbike.

'That's not a motorbike. It's a chicken chaser,'
said Rob when he saw Wesley on the bike.

'You couldn't catch chickens on it.'

'I don't want to catch chickens.

I just deliver pizzas,' said Wesley.

But the bike was old and slow.

Once a kid on a push-bike had overtaken him.

A man pushing a wheelbarrow
had even beaten him up a steep hill once.
'Get off and push it,' the man had shouted.
But Wesley didn't care.
'It's fast enough for me,' he said.
'It's too slow to catch a cold,' said Rob.

Wesley loved his job. Beppe who owned
the pizza shop would shout:
'Two deep-pan mushroom and cheese.
Twenty-nine Hardwick Road.'
Wesley had his bike parked up ready.
Then he was off. Threading his way
through a mass of little streets.
He knew all the streets around town.
He never got lost.
Every time the customers had their pizzas
ready to eat in 15 minutes.
Sometimes it took less time.
'The 15-minute kid'
was the nickname Beppe gave him.

He'd just finished a deep-pan delivery
when Rob came into the shop.
'You'll never believe it,' he said.
'What?'
'They're starting up youth nights at speedway.
You can have a go round the track.
Ride real speedway bikes.'
Wesley gave him a hard look.
'You said you'd had enough of speedway.'
'Yea. Well this is different,' said Rob.
'It will be a real laugh. Are you coming?'
'I have to work tomorrow night.'
'We can go after you finish work.
It won't be too late.'

3

Jed

By the time they got to the speedway track
it was late. The stadium was empty.
Nobody was around.
'Too late,' said Wesley.
But the big metal gates were still open.
Rob walked in through them.
'Anybody around?' he shouted.
Nobody answered.
'Leave it Rob,' said Wesley.

At the end of the track was a speedway bike.
Rob looked at its thick chunky tyres
and gave them a kick.
'Don't,' said Wesley.
Rob looked the bike all over.
'It's a beauty,' he said.
'We'd better go,' said Wesley glancing round.
Then Rob climbed onto the bike.
'Feel the power,' he said.
'Nought to 70 in three seconds.
No brakes. No mercy.'

'Just earth flying behind you.
Up into the air as you burn up the track.'

'Hey you. Get off that bike,' shouted a voice.
Wesley looked towards the clubhouse.
Jed Black, the club's leading rider,
was walking towards them.
Rob was sitting on his bike
in his own dream world.
'Down to the first bend. Lean into the bend.
Pull the bike round. Get your foot
out onto the track,' he said to himself.

'Rob get off that bike. It's Jed's bike.'
But Rob was still in his speedway dream.
'Hear the crowd roar,' he said.
Jed was right by him now.
'Get off my bike,' he said quietly.
Rob climbed off the bike.
'You want to be a speedway rider?' asked Jed.
'Yea,' said Rob.
'Then come to youth night.
Next Thursday at half past seven.'

4

First Race

Thursday nights couldn't come around
quick enough.
Wesley now did an early shift at Beppe's.
Then it was onto the chicken chaser
and up to the stadium.
On with the goggles, gloves and helmet.
Then climb up onto a real bike.
They'd been going round the track
learning how to handle the bike and
slide round corners.
They'd done this for quite a few weeks.

'Time for your first small race,' said Jed.
'Two laps of the track.
A few more youths will be joining in.
We want to see how you go.
But remember safety comes first.
Always think safety.'
Rob and Wesley and a lad called Ben
were in the first heat.
'A fourth rider will join you in the race,'
said Jed.

They sat on their bikes
waiting by the starting tape.
They tried to keep cool.
But still the fourth bike didn't join them.
'Come on. Come on,' shouted Jed.
At last they could hear a bike behind them.
A black bike blasted up the track.
On the bike was a rider in silver gear
wearing a silver helmet and silver goggles.

'Ready to start,' said Jed
over the loud speaker.
The starting light went green
and the tape went up.
The race had started.
The face in the silver helmet
shot past Wesley.
It was into the bend and going like a dream.
It went past Ben and then past Rob.
The silver rider on the black bike was flying.
It did the two laps in less than a minute.
It beat all of them by miles.

The silver rider went into the next race
as well – and the next.
It beat them all and won every race.
'The winner is number six – the silver flier,'
said Jed on the loud speaker.
'Who is it?' said Rob.
'What a demon,' said Ben.

The black bike did a lap of honour
then stopped by the loud speaker.

'Congratulations to Zena,' said Jed
on the loud speaker. 'Three great wins.'
Zena's helmet was taken off
and the goggles removed.
They saw Zena's face for the first time.
They had all been beaten by a girl.

5

Zena

'A girl,' said Rob.

'A girl beat us all,' said Ben.

'Have you ever seen a girl ride in speedway?' asked Elroy.

'No. Never,' said all 11 beaten riders.

'Have you ever seen a girl play in the Premier Football League?' asked Liam.

'No. Never,' said all 11 beaten riders.

'She must have cheated,' said Ranjit.

'Yes. She must have cheated,' agreed all the lads.

'It was luck,' said Josh.

'Sure it was luck,' said Elroy.

'She had a winning place in the line up
at the start. She always raced on the inside.
Anybody can win on the inside.'

'Yes. Anybody can win on the inside,'
said Andy.

'We'll show her,' said Rob.

The lads tried to show her
for the next three weeks.

They raced hard. She raced harder.

They forced her to start on the outside.

'The outside is the best place to start,' she said.

They tried to put her off. They failed.

'I'm going to knock her off the track,' said Rob.

He smashed his bike into a wall.

Zena zoomed past him
and won the race in record time.

'This is hopeless,' he said.

All the lads agreed.

6

Dirty Tricks

Later, Jed said to them all:
'At the next speedway night
there will be a special event.
You can all enter and the winner
will then be able to race for the club.
It's a chance to ride in premier speedway.'

'We know who the winner will be,' said Ben.
'Miss Silver Speed,' said Elroy.
'No,' said Rob.
'No?' they all asked.

'It's not Zena but her bike,' said Rob.
'If we can knock out her bike
we can knock out her.'
'Knock her out?' asked Wesley.
They turned on him.
'Yea. Knock her out …
and you are going to lead us to the gold.'
'Gold? What gold?'
'Her bike of course,' said Rob.
'You know where she lives. Don't you?'
'Do I?'

It was true. Wesley had delivered a pizza
to her house a few weeks before.
'Do you?' asked the rest.
This was getting ugly.
Wesley didn't want any part of it.
'No,' he said.
'Liar,' said Rob. 'You liar.'
Then three of them grabbed hold of him
and swung him upside down.
They held his face
a centimetre from the ground.

'Where does she live?'
Wesley was terrified.
'Tell us or we'll drop you head first.'
He had to tell them the address.
He just had to. They swung him back upright.
'Good,' said Rob.
'And now you can take us to her house.
Like you were delivering a pizza.
Only it'll be you in a deep pan
if you don't take us right to her house.'
Wesley climbed onto the old chicken chaser.
Only he was the chicken.
He was too scared to ride off
or do anything about this stupidity.

They soon got to her house.
'Now knock on the door.
Like you had a pizza,' said Rob.
Wesley's knees wobbled as he climbed
up the steps which led to her house.
He knocked on the door. Nobody answered.
'Knock again,' shouted Rob from the road.
Wesley knocked a second time. Still no answer.

'There's nobody in.'
'Perfect,' said Rob. 'Just what we need.
A bit of peace and quiet for our little job.'
Then he grabbed Wesley by the arm
and pulled it behind his back.
Wesley yelled out in pain.
'Just tell us where she keeps her bike
and I'll let go. It's as easy as that Wesley.'
'No,' shouted Wesley.
'I'm not helping you any more.'
Rob pulled his arm harder.
'Come on Wesley,' he said

Wesley's arm hurt bad
but he was not going to help him.
He couldn't believe that Rob
was supposed to be his mate.
'Let him be,' said Elroy.
'It's bound to be round here somewhere.'
Some of them went into the garden.
Rob still had Wesley's arm round his back.
'Don't want the chicken to run off,' he said.

'Rob … Rob … in here,' shouted Elroy.
Rob pulled Wesley into the garden.
'In here Rob.'

Wesley was dragged past a big tree
and through bushes.
Behind the bushes was a wall.
The wall led to a shed.
Standing in the middle of the shed
was Zena's gleaming black bike.

'Just look at that,' said Rob.
'What a bike,' said Ben.
'Must be a few quid's worth here,' said Elroy.
'Fancy wheels,' said Rob.
'Smart tyres,' said Ben.
'Nice gear,' said Ranjit.
'Cool machine,' said Liam.
'So polished,' said Rob.

Elroy found a hammer on a bench
and swung it in his hand.
'What a pity to spoil it,' he said.

Liam found a big spanner on the floor.
'A shame to smash it,' he said.'
'But we can't have a girl winning all the time.'
'It's not the girl it's the bike,'
said Rob moving closer to the motorbike.

Elroy and Liam moved closer too.
Elroy smashed the hammer down on its seat.
'No,' shouted Rob pulling the hammer
out of Elroy's hand.'
'We are going to do something
far more clever than that.
Something she won't know about
until she starts the race.'

Wesley had to take his chance.
Rob had let go of his arm.
It was now or never.
The door of the shed was open.
He ran. He ran out of that open door.
He went through the bushes
and past the big tree.
Then he ran down the steps and into the road.
The chicken chaser was ready.
He jumped onto the seat
and turned on the engine.
Without looking back he rode away
like a scared chicken all the way back home.

7

The Big Race

The stadium was full. A big crowd
had come to see a good night's speedway.
The floodlights shone brightly.
'This is a special race,'
said the loud speaker.
'The young person who wins this race
will join our top team.'
Wesley gripped his motorbike throttle.
Four bikes were at the starting tape.
One of them was black
with a rider wearing silver.

Wesley wanted to shout out:
'Look out Zena. Your bike is fixed.'
But it was too late.
The chicken had been too scared to warn her.

The starting light went to green.
The tape went up. Off zoomed the bikes.
Zena was first into the bend
and first out of it.
Now she turned her throttle to full power.
Faster and faster she rode.
'Look out Zena. Look out,'
said Wesley to himself.

They were into the second bend.
Zena was in the middle of the track.
There was space on the inside.
Space for a rider to cut through the gap.
Rob saw the gap straight away.
His bike drew level with Zena's.
'Look out Zena.'
His bike was so close. Too close for safety.
'Look out.'

The wheels of Zena and Rob's bike touched.
Then there was a crunch and a big cloud
of flying dirt.
SMASH!
Something hit the barrier. A bike had crashed.
The cloud of dirt cleared.
The twisted heap of a motorbike
lay on the dirt.
A person stumbled away from the heap.
'Zena!' shouted Wesley.

But the silver rider on the black bike
was still riding round the track.
It was Rob who had crashed.
They stopped the race.
Rob was taken to hospital in an ambulance.
Wesley went over to Zena.
'They fixed your bike so you would crash.
But you're okay.'
'Oh that,' said Zena in a cool voice.
'You knew about it?' said Wesley.
'Yes. Good riders always check their bikes
before a race. Safety comes first.
You lads had better remember that.'

At the next speedway race night
the Reds will have a new rider.
You can be sure Zena
will be up there with the best.